The Wish Fairy

The Biggest, Bestest Fish Ever!

An original children's story
By Sandra Reilly

First Printing 2017
Copyright © 2016 by Sandra Reilly

www.sandrareilly.com

Library of Congress Cataloging-in-Publication Data
Reilly, Sandra/The Wish Fairy: The Biggest, Bestest
Fish Ever

Summary: Magical adventures of a bungling Wish
Fairy, her friend Hope, and a very special fishing
adventure.
ISBN 978-0-9964299-6-2

I. Reilly, Sandra 1948- II. Title TXu 2-027-104
III. Book Covers VAu 1-285-320

I would like to dedicate this book to a very special man in my life; my Uncle Ernie Derminio. He was not only my uncle; he was my godfather and godfather to my daughter. He was a special type of person and was larger than life. You could not help smiling when you were in his presence. He had a great sense of humor and was there for me at every special occasion in my life, even though he would say he couldn't attend because he was going to be at North Lake (every single time). He would always say that he disliked children and to keep them away from him, and yet he was key in developing a youth bowling league, was a deputy sheriff, and drove a school bus. My Uncle Ernie would have encouraged me to continue writing these books. I love and miss him very much.

Two of the main characters in my story, James and Greg, were created in honor of my loving father-in-law James, who welcomed me into his heart and home like his own daughter, and my nephew Greg, who was a fun loving and kind young man who was taken from us way too soon.

Another character, Greg's mother Marlene was created in honor of my Aunt Marlene, who is not only my friend and confidant, but also my editor. It is due to her endless hard work that my stories have merit and are so enjoyable.

I also cannot thank my husband Jeff enough for the hours of work he puts in to promoting my books. He is my rock and my biggest fan. He is always there to tell me to keep writing and to have faith in my abilities.

My stories come alive on the pages of my Wish Fairy books because of the endless encouragement that I receive from my family and friends, and for that I am forever grateful.

Before you begin...

Throughout my Wish Fairy book series, you will come to love the little girl named Hope. I would like to tell you a little bit about her so you can get to know her better.

She lives in upstate New York with her mother. She is a country girl, with a very active imagination, and is a firm believer in magic. Hope is a very loving and caring 8-year-old who loves her flowers of the field, and for good reason. You will come to know her as a good friend of Misty, the Wish Fairy. Whenever Misty is in trouble, Hope is the one she goes to for help.

Another character you will come to know in this series is Hope's mother, Mary Catherine. She is a down to earth, hard working woman. She has faith in her daughter but needs a little time and help to believe that magic really exists. A pure of heart person, she becomes a true fighter for what is right and magical. She also gives Hope advice and, together, they plan the best way to grant wishes.

In this story you will meet a wonderful family who lives in Lake George, New York, a lake in the Adirondack Mountains. This family has fallen on hard times, trying to keep their fishing excursion business going after a bad storm damages their boat. Will their faith and belief in their Wish Fairy help them through this difficult time, or will some strange lake creatures get in the way?

I hope you will learn to love Misty (the sometimes not so perfect, always getting into trouble, kind of fairy), her friends, and all the characters that live in both her world and ours.

The Wish Fairy

The Biggest, Bestest Fish Ever

Sandra Reilly

Hope is a dreamer; she looks at things differently than everyone else. She is an eight-year-old girl who lives with her mom in upstate New York. She has a very active imagination and is a pure of heart believer in magic. Hope has had more than her share of adventure and excitement, mainly due to the fact that she has a bungling, not so perfect Wish Fairy as her best friend.

Hope was able to convince her mother and the whole entire village that magic does exist and that fairies do live beneath the ground, where her favorite wildflowers grow.

It was by this very wildflower field that Hope loved to sit. She would often gaze out her window and look out over the field just waiting for the first buds of spring to appear. She knew that it was the fairies that did the planting and the baby fairies that did the painting, and she just couldn't wait to see the field come alive again. It would be spring soon, and Hope could see the tiny buds starting on the trees. She loved how the warm, gentle, spring breeze made everything smell so fresh and clean. It had been a long, hard winter, and the fairies sure had their work cut out for them if the field was to look beautiful for the villagers.

Hope looked up at the sky as the sound of an airplane flying overhead brought her out of the beautiful daydream that she was having. She was remembering the night that her little friend Misty became a Wish Fairy. The fairy Queen had placed two rainbows in the sky and, as everyone watched, the two rainbows combined to make the most beautiful rainbow anyone had ever seen. This was the Queen's message that the two worlds, the world of the fairy kingdom and the human race, were now combined as one, just as the rainbows had been.

Her mother, Mary Catherine, came into the room and told Hope that it was time for lunch. She said, "Hope, it is such a beautiful day, would you like to eat outside on the porch?"

"Oh, yes, Mom," said Hope. "That will be so much fun."

They ate their sandwiches that were made from the jelly they had canned in the fall. The berries were so sweet and the bread so fresh that Hope thought she had never tasted anything so delicious.

"Holy Fairy Dust, Mom, these are the best sandwiches ever."

"Thank you, Hope. Now finish your milk, please."

They finished off their lunch with some homemade oatmeal raisin cookies and spent a few minutes just talking and enjoying each other's company. Mary Catherine got up, Hope helped her clean the table, and her mother went into the house to do some sewing. Hope called to her mom and said, "I think I would like to take a walk into town. Do you think that would be ok?"

"Sure," her mom said. "Go and enjoy yourself." Even though it was a short walk into town, her mom watched out the window until Hope reached the village green.

As she walked along the small creek that led into town, Hope stopped to watch the squirrels playing, their bushy tails bouncing up and down as they chased each other through the branches of the chestnut tree. She stopped to say hello to the couples that were walking hand in hand enjoying the day and then found an empty park bench where she sat down.

It was so calm and peaceful there that, at first, she didn't notice the people who were sitting across the path from her on a similar park bench. Holy Fairy Dust! The thought popped into her head that it had been awhile since she had spoken to her little friend Misty. I hope she contacts me soon, thought Hope. She realized that they hadn't seen each other since their Ireland adventure. She smiled to herself and knew that it wouldn't be long before Misty would come to her with a problem involving a new wish that she had to grant.

Hope finally took a look at the people sitting across from her. They looked very familiar, but she couldn't quite remember where she knew them from. Then she realized that she didn't know them at all. They just reminded her of some people she saw every summer at Lake George in the Adirondack Mountains. A friend of Hope's mom has a beautiful home there, and each year on summer vacation they would visit. She remembered them as a grandfather and grandson and that the grandfather had a fishing excursion boat that was docked not far from the house where Hope and her mom visited. She would talk to the grandfather, James, and he would tell her all about the people that came from all over to hire his boat for a day of fishing. She loved the stories he told about the different kinds of fish they caught. He would show her pictures of the small and large mouth bass, the northern pike, and the trout that his passengers would catch.

Greg, she knew, was his young grandson's name. He was a tall boy for 10, with brown hair and brown eyes. He wore glasses and, when he got nervous about something, he would keep pushing his glasses up on his nose. Hope asked him one summer day why he followed his grandfather around like a puppy dog. He smiled and pointed to a large sign that hung over the bait and tackle shop. The sign said, "GRANDPOP AND ME FISHING EXCURSIONS INQUIRE HERE."

Hope remembered that the boat was a beauty, and the name ELIZABETH was written in bright red letters along the side. She found out from Greg that Elizabeth was his grandmother's name, and his grandfather wanted it on the boat as a reminder of how much he loved her. She had passed away about three years ago and now there was just Greg, his grandfather, James, and his mom, Marlene. Greg's dad had passed away when he was just a baby, so he had become very close to his grandfather. They were a small, but very happy family.

The fishing business took care of the bills and upkeep to the large 26-foot boat, and Greg's mother made fish chowder and cheddar biscuits that she supplied to the local restaurants on the wharf. That took care of most of the day-to-day expenses, but there was never much money left over for extra things.

Thinking about her two summer friends made Hope smile. "Holy Fairy Dust, I really miss those two! Here it is barely spring and already I can't wait to go to Lake George."

She didn't realize how long she had been sitting on that bench, but the weather started to change. It turned colder, and small drops of rain started to fall. Hope got up and ran as fast as she could back to her house.

As the days got longer and warmer, Hope would sit under the big oak tree in the middle of the wildflower field and watch as, little by little, the flowers grew more and more beautiful. She would gaze at the ground and remember the time that she and her mother were allowed to speak to the High Council of Fairies at this very spot. It was when her friend Misty was trying to earn the right to become a Wish Fairy. She needed the help of Hope and her mother to convince the Queen that she was worthy of such an important position in the fairy kingdom.

Holy Fairy Dust! What an exciting time that was. This memory also reminded Hope that she hadn't talked to her friend in a while. She wasn't upset, because she knew that there were a lot of people counting on Misty to grant their wishes. And besides, Hope knew that Misty could never go too long without visiting her best friend.

Just as if Hope had called upon her, Misty appeared out of nowhere, landed on a large blade of grass, and said "Hi, Hope. Did you miss me?" Hope could see the corners of her friend's mouth turn up into a great big smile.

"Misty, I am so glad to see you. I have been thinking about you a lot lately."

"Well, here I am, Hope, and we really need to talk." Oh, no, thought Hope. Here it comes. Misty must have a problem with a wish that she needs to grant.

"Hope," said Misty, "don't you go to Lake George in the summertime to visit your mom's friend?"

"Yes, Misty, why do you ask?"

"Well, I received a wish from a very

special little boy named Gregory."

"Yes, I know who he is. His grandfather, James, has a fishing boat that he hires out to the tourists."

"Not any more, he doesn't," said Misty sadly.

"Why, what do you mean?"

Misty went on to explain to her friend that after she and her mother left at the end of August last year, a terrible hurricane type storm came up the Atlantic coast and into New York, hitting Lake George and many surrounding areas in the Adirondack Mountains. Many large boats were damaged, destroyed, and even sunk.

"Oh, no!" cried Hope. "Are you telling me that James' boat was sunk?"

"No, but it was damaged — a lot. He cannot use it as it is."

Misty hugged Hope and told her that Greg's wish was very, very worthy, and she wanted to do her best to grant it. She also told her friend that it was not going to be easy, and she was going to need Hope's help for sure.

"Holy Fairy Dust!" said Hope. "I can feel another adventure coming on."

Hope carried Misty on her shoulder as she walked back to the house. Mary Catherine was busy, as usual, washing windows and doing spring cleaning. She had all the windows open, because she loved the way the house smelled with the warm air coming through. She saw Misty and Hope coming up the walk and decided to take a break. She knew something was troubling them by the looks on their faces. She knew these two well enough that it probably had something to do with a wish.

When they got on the porch, she said, "Come, sit down. It looks like we need to have a talk."

Hope sat on the porch swing next to her mom, and Misty sat in the little pink flowered tea cup that Mary Catherine had lined with soft material, just for Misty.

When Misty explained to Mary Catherine what had happened to James' boat, she couldn't believe it. The three of them sat on that porch for a very long time, talking about Lake George, Greg, and his grandfather. Hope's mom started the conversation by saying how much they enjoyed spending their summers at the lake.

She told Misty that from the big wrap around porch they could see the Blue Mountains surrounding the lake and how the lake sparkled in the sunlight. The water was so pure that it was piped right into the homes for the people who lived there to enjoy. "The people are so friendly," Hope's mother said. She loved to walk through the village and buy the goodies that the local store owners had for sale. She especially loved the fish chowder and cheddar biscuits at the wharf restaurant. "In fact, Misty, it is Greg's mother, Marlene, who supplies the chowder and biscuits to the restaurant."

Hope told Misty that she loved walking from the house, in Lake George, to the boat dock to visit Greg and James. On the way she would stop and sit on a beautifully carved wooden bench that one of the fishermen had made and left on the path for the tourists to sit on. It was beautiful. On the back were carvings of all the beautiful fish that lived in the lake.

The path was Hope's favorite place to walk because of all the brightly colored wildflowers that lined both sides of the cobblestone walkway. Every time she would walk down that path she would think to herself, "Holy Fairy Dust. There must be fairies that live here also. These flowers are growing wild, and look at the colors." She could see purple iris, bright yellow goldenrod, and pure white Queen Anne's lace. Who else but the babies could have painted anything so beautiful? (The babies were the youngest members of the fairy kingdom where Misty lived and were responsible for painting all the flowers.)

Hope told Misty that she had often talked to Greg and that he had never mentioned the fact that he believed in the Wish Fairy. Misty said he believed because his grandfather would tell him stories about the fairies. Greg believed in magic, but it was his grandmother who was the true believer. James had just told Greg the summer before about the Wish Fairy and how she had granted a wish for his grandmother when she was a small child. "Maybe it was something that he just didn't want to share with anyone," thought Hope.

Hope remembered one hot sunny day in late July. They had only been at the lake for about a week and a day. She had watched James' fishing boat sail up to the dock to unload some happy tourists with their day's catch of fish. She knew they would be there for at least two hours before they took off again with a new load of people, so she ran down to the dock to talk to her friends before they left again.

Hope got there just as Greg was finishing up his chores. He was about to take a break, and she asked him if he would like to walk down the wharf with her and get some ice cold frozen lemonade — her treat. He said he would love to. "So," she told Misty. "There we were, sitting on the dock eating our lemon ice, watching the seagulls as they swooped down to try to get some morsel of food that a tourist had dropped." I told Greg how much I loved this place and that I felt like I was really beginning to get to know it. He told me that I only knew what all the other tourists knew. Then he asked me if I wanted to hear some real things about the lake that only the locals knew.

Naturally, I said, of course, and Greg started talking.

Mary Catherine asked Misty if she would like to tell them about the wish now, but Misty said she wanted to hear what Greg said to Hope on that day. She thought that maybe there would be a clue in their conversation that would help Misty grant his wish. So Hope picked up where she left off in her talk with Greg.

"I asked him what he meant when he said I only knew what the tourists knew. He replied that there was a lot to this lake that only a very few people knew. There were stories and legends that dated back from when his grandfather was a small boy."

"Interesting," said Misty. "What else did he say?"

Hope said he told her that the lake was about 200 feet deep, and there were rock shelves where huge fish were said to live.

These shelves were in a dangerous area, so unless you grew up here and knew the lake by heart, only the very foolish tourist would try to fish near the shelves. He said that Lake George was known as the Queen of the Adirondacks, and she ruled over her community, like any good leader. That is why when the weather turns really bad, legend says it is because someone or something has angered the Queen. When the weather is beautiful and warm, legend says it is because the Queen is happy and brings hundreds of tourists into the community to boat and fish and swim.

Hope said that the best part about her talk with Greg was when he told her about the Biggest, Bestest Fish contest. It was held every year, bringing to Lake George hundreds of fishermen and families from all over the country. The prize was a whopping $20,000. Grandpop and Me Fishing Excursions had taken plenty of fishermen out on the lake during the contest, but none of them wanted to venture near the shelves. The tourists had heard the locals talk of a water creature that they called the monster in the lake.

"Really!" exclaimed Misty. "A monster?"

"That's what the locals say," said Hope.

Mary Catherine just sat there with her hands folded in her lap as Hope was talking. She had a very sad look on her face. "I feel so bad for those people. Maybe I should call my friend and ask her how we can help and if there is anything that we can bring that will help them. We will be leaving for the lake in a few days, and I just don't know what to expect or how to help."

Misty flew over to Hope's mom and said, "Don't worry. Let me tell you about Greg's wish and maybe you can help figure out how you can help. As for me, I am going to have my hands full granting this wish. Well, one good thing, at least I won't have to worry about the troll trying to stop me this time."

Misty had no idea how wrong she was.

Misty began telling her friends about Greg's wish. She had just been called to the castle by the Queen, and she was almost there when she felt a flutter in her wish basket. "Oh, no!" she thought to herself. "This is the worst possible moment to have a wish appear." She had no idea what the Queen wanted, and now she was going to have to stop and read this wish. After all, she was told over and over by her mother (who was also a Wish Fairy), the Fairy Council, and the Queen, that no matter what, wishes always come first.

She landed on a tree limb that was just about five feet above the area where the groomers were braiding the unicorn's mane. Even though she wanted more than anything to just sit and watch the groomers, she opened her basket and began to read.

Misty told Hope that Greg started out by saying that he loved the idea of having a Wish Fairy. She could tell that he was a sensitive, loving, and pure of heart boy by looking at the dried tears that had stained the paper the wish was written on. He was so scared that if he wished and the wish failed, then he would be letting down someone that he loved with his whole heart. He said that he was almost afraid to wish but, after listening to the stories that his grandfather had told him about fairies, he changed his mind. How brave he was to have so much faith and trust.

To him, his wish was simple. He explained to Misty that his grandfather's boat had been damaged, and he didn't know how to help him get it repaired. She guessed that there was a lot more to this wish and decided to visit him that very night. But first she had to keep her appointment with the Queen and explain why she was late, again.

"That went well," thought Misty. The Queen had wanted to know if she would like to host a party for the new wish fairies. She thought Misty was the perfect one to talk to them about what a Wish Fairy should and should not do. Although the Queen said it with a smile on her face, Misty knew that she was very serious. The Queen told Misty to go and grant the wish in her basket and to try not to get in any trouble.

Of course, Greg's window was not open. That would have been way too easy. Now Misty had to figure out another way to get into Greg's room. She could see him sleeping peacefully, from her spot in the tree outside his window. She was just going to have to stick it out until she could find a way in. Once she was in his room, she would have to appear without scaring the poor boy. Gee, this Wish Fairy thing was not easy.

As she sat outside Greg's window, she

thought about what she had seen while flying over the village. It wasn't the total destruction that she expected, but it was definitely bad. Some of the businesses were still boarded up. Many ships were repaired and running, but a lot of them were out of the water just sitting on trailers.

One in particular caught her eye. It was a beautiful boat, tipped on its side. There was one gaping hole where it looked like the mast of another ship had plowed into it. One side looked fine from what she could see. She also saw that there was a name written across it in bright red letters. It said simply: ELIZABETH. She had a feeling that was the boat that belonged to Greg's grandfather, James.

Greg opened his eyes slowly, then shot straight up in bed rubbing his eyes. Was he dreaming? Was his imagination running wild? But no, he was fully awake now, and there right on the edge of his window sill, outside, was a little fairy peeking in. When Misty saw Greg looking at her, she put on her brightest smile and waved at him to open the window. He smiled back at her. He just couldn't believe it. She was really here. He had called upon his Wish Fairy, and here she was.

He opened the window, and Misty flew in and landed on his pillow. "Hi, Greg," she said as she patted the bed next to where she was sitting. "Come, sit down. Let me introduce myself. I am Misty, and I am your Wish Fairy. I have come to find out what it is that you want me to do for you. I read your wish, and I got the impression that there were things you weren't telling me. Am I right?"

"Yes," he said. "There is so much I need to tell you that I don't know where to begin."

"Try at the beginning and we will take it from there."

Misty looked at Hope and Mary Catherine with tears in her eyes. She said that this little boy's wish came straight from his heart. The story he told me is very sad, and I have to grant this wish. He went on to say that his grandfather's business started to slow down a little bit at the beginning of August. Several of the tourists were heading home early, because the weather had not been good and the fish were not cooperating either.

Money was tight, so his grandfather had to make some hard choices. One of them was that he decided to cancel his insurance on the boat, because he could no longer afford it. Then the hurricane type storm hit, his boat was badly damaged, and he had no extra money for repairs. Greg's mom, Marlene, did all she could to help by selling her homemade fish chowder and biscuits but, with the lack of tourists, even the restaurants that always ordered from her had stopped buying.

Greg went from house to house doing odd chores, painting, fixing fences, hammering up shutters that the strong wind had knocked down, and any odd job that he could find. But, it was not enough. If they couldn't get the boat repaired before the busy fishing season began, his grandfather would have to put the boat up for sale. Then what would they do?

Misty told Greg to try not to worry, because she was going to do everything in her power to grant his wish. He just needed to have faith in her. Secretly, she hoped that she wouldn't let him down.

"Oh Misty," said Hope. "Holy Fairy Dust, what are you going to do? We all know that wish fairies cannot use money to directly grant a wish, and it looks like that is exactly what Greg needs — money."

"I know, Hope, but you gave me an idea."

"Me? Yay, what is it?"

"Remember when you were telling me about the conversation you had with Greg?"

"Yes, I remember."

"Well, you mentioned a fishing contest with a lot of prize money for the winner. What if Greg was to catch the biggest, bestest fish ever? Then he would get the prize money, and they could fix the boat so Grandpop and Me Fishing Excursions would be back in business."

"That is a great idea," said Mary Catherine and Hope at the same time. "But how can we be sure Greg will catch the biggest fish?" said Hope.

"Well, that's how I will be granting Greg's wish."

"Holy Fairy Dust!" said Hope. "This just might work."

Little did they know what kind of trouble they were in for.

Misty told Hope that she was leaving now to say good-bye to her mother, and then she would be heading back to Lake George. She wanted to do some research on the rock shelves and the fish that lived there. She told Hope that she would be in touch as soon as she knew something. If not, she would see her when she and her mom arrived at the lake. The two friends hugged good-bye, and Misty flew off out of the window.

In the short time it took Hope and her Mom to pack up to go to Lake George, Hope thought of a hundred reasons why this wish could go wrong. She had been around Misty long enough to know that no wish was easy to grant, and that's what made them so special. She hoped that, like all the other wishes she helped her friend with, they would be able to overcome any evil or trouble that came their way. Although, it was with a sigh of relief that she remembered that the evil troll was safely tucked away in an Irish prison surrounded by chamomile plants. (These are the plants that Misty learned would cause a troll to become very weak.) "Or was he?" thought Hope. "We thought we were rid of him many times before. Holy Fairy Dust! Why do I have the feeling we have not heard the last of him? Or is there something even worse out there waiting to stop Misty?"

The day Hope and her mom left for the lake was bright and sunny. Hope considered this a good sign. She couldn't wait to get there. They had heard from her mom's friend that most of the cleanup had been done by the many volunteers that poured into the village to help. There were only a few boats left stranded. The village, Hope learned, was getting ready for the big fishing contest. Hope wondered what plan Misty had come up with to help Greg catch the biggest fish.

They arrived at about two o'clock in the afternoon. Hope couldn't wait to see Greg and James. She saw them sitting on the dock and could tell that they were not acting like the same people she left last summer. They were sitting in their Adirondack chairs, staring out at the lake. She could usually find them on the dock, busy doing something to get ready for the next fishing trip.

Greg's pole was not in the water where he always kept it. It was leaning up against the bait and tackle building. She wanted to cry as she watched the small boy grab his grandfather's hand when the old man looked up at the sign on the building. Hope read the sign and understood their pain. Over the original sign that said, GRANDPOP AND ME FISHING EXCURSIONS INQUIRE WITHIN, there was a large red banner that said CLOSED UNTIL FURTHUR NOTICE DUE TO HIGH WIND AND STORM DAMAGE.

"Oh, no," thought Hope, "what can I possibly say to these two wonderful friends? Hope wanted to run back to the house as fast as she could but knew that this is not what friends do. Friends stand by each other no matter what. "Holy Fairy Dust, I sure hope Misty has some good news for us."

It was as if Mary Catherine could read her daughter's mind. She put on a light jacket and decided to go down to the dock and see how things were going. She knew that Hope was having a hard time dealing with all these sad feelings.

Hope needed some time to think, so she stopped for a little bit, and that gave Mary Catherine time to catch up with her daughter. "Hi, Hope. What ya doin'?"

"Hi, Mom. I am so glad to see you. I am

having a hard time walking over to see Greg and James. I don't know what to say."

"Oh, Hope, you don't need any fancy words to say to them, just be yourself and speak from your heart."

Greg turned around, sensing that someone was there. His grandfather spotted them too and got up from his chair. They both started waving frantically for Hope and her mom to come over. The friends hugged, and they went to sit down on the picnic table in the shade. After they finished their small talk about what they had been doing and how everyone was feeling, Hope's mom decided to bring up the subject of the hurricane type storm and the loss of their boat.

Greg wanted to show Hope the boat and the gaping hole in the side. As the two children skipped off hand in hand, the two adults settled back into their chairs with glasses of iced tea. Mary Catherine started off by asking

James what happened. He said that shortly after they left for home last August, he was getting ready to take one of the last excursions of the day out on the lake. He always had a good sense of when a storm was brewing, but this one took him totally by surprise. He said that he barely got out of the cove when the wind starting whipping up. Thinking the worse, he turned his boat around, went back to shore, and told the tourists to go to their hotels and cabins and wait for instructions. He knew that this was going to be a bad one.

He had just enough time to throw down the anchor and get himself and Greg off the boat before he noticed the sky. First it turned bright red-orange like fire and then pitch black like night. The wind was so strong that they struggled to reach the basement of the bait and tackle shop. They arrived just as the golf ball sized hail smashed to the ground. They could hear pieces of furniture, small trees, and every other kind of debris hit the building. The wind was deafening, and Greg held his hands over his ears. He kept shouting to his grandfather, "The boat, Pop, the boat! What is going to happen to the boat?"

Greg knew that they hadn't had time to put it into a boat shelter before the storm hit. Hope's mother couldn't believe what she was hearing. She had so many questions. She stopped him. "Oh, James, I am so sorry. It must have been terrifying for all of you."

"It was," said James, "but I had to keep calm for Greg. My poor grandson was worried sick about his mama, but I knew that my daughter, Marlene, lived by the water long enough to know when she needed to get to a storm shelter. All throughout the storm, Greg and I were hoping that the boat would survive the strong hurricane like winds. We needed to hold on to our faith that, if it was damaged, it wouldn't be so bad that we couldn't get it repaired."

Mary Catherine then asked James if he knew that Greg had called upon his Wish Fairy for help. He said no, that he had no idea that his grandson had done that. She told him about Greg's wish. The old man got so quiet that Mary Catherine was afraid to look at him. He was openly crying. He said that his wish would be that everyone would have someone to love them as much as Greg loved him.

"I have another question, if that is okay?" asked Hope's mom.

"Sure, what is it?"

"Greg told Misty that you canceled the insurance on your boat. I am just curious. Why would you cancel the insurance on your boat? Isn't that an important thing to have?"

"It is, as I am finding out now. Let me explain to you why I was forced to make that difficult decision."

As James was about to speak, he noticed

Greg and Hope walking down the pier toward them. He decided to wait for them before he continued. James began. "For the last few weeks before you and Hope left the lake, business starting dropping off. The fish were not biting, and the tourists didn't want to spend their money taking a big boat out, so they just sat fishing off the docks."

"At first, it was a slight change. Then we began to notice that when Greg and I went out fishing, we couldn't get the catch that we needed to sell to the markets and restaurants in town. Business was down, and I just could not afford to pay the insurance any more. I was hoping things would pick up and, when it did, I would get the insurance back on my boat."

"It is really strange. All of a sudden, it was as if something was scaring the fish away."

"Oh, we know what that was, right Pop?" Greg jumped right into the conversation.

"Now, Greg, we talked about this. You

know that the fisherman's tale about the mermaid curse and the monster in the lake was just started last year."

"I know, Grandpop, but wouldn't that explain the sightings and the lack of fish?"

"Whoa, wait a minute," said Hope. "Holy Fairy Dust! Is there a tale that you haven't told me about? Is it magical? Because I believe in anything magical! Did you say mermaid? I always wanted to see one of those. I have seen many mystical creatures, but never a mermaid."

"Slow down, young lady," said James. "We will answer all of your questions."

James had Hope's attention now. She sat straight up in her chair and paid full attention to what James was saying. She did not want to miss a single word. He said that right around the same time the fish began to get scarce, there had been some strange sightings. Something was out in the deepest part of the lake. No one had seen the thing up close, but there were a few fishermen who said the thing had come close enough to their boats to be visible, but not close enough to identify. Some tourists said that they had seen it and that it was indeed an ugly sight. Some insisted that it was just a huge fish that lives up under one of the rock shelves.

"What about the mermaid? Where does she come into this story?"

"Well, Hope, this is how the fishermen tell it."

As James was telling his story to Hope, Greg, and Mary Catherine, nobody noticed the little fairy sitting in the flower box in the tackle shop window. Misty was listening very carefully to everything that Greg's grandfather was saying. She wasn't exactly sure yet how it was going to fit in with her plan to grant Greg's wish, but she had a feeling that there might be some very important clues hidden in this story.

A very cold feeling crept over her body, and she shivered. She couldn't help but think that this is how she felt whenever the evil troll was around. But that couldn't be, could it?

James continued his story. He told them that the tale started a year ago. The old folks that gathered in the diner every morning for coffee said that the story started when a stranger who had been sailing on the lake stopped at the village and ran into the diner. He began telling a strange story about a mermaid that had appeared out of the water. He said that she asked him for help to save her sister. The man, thinking that he was seeing things, decided to go right on by without helping. On his way back through, he got hung up on some rocks and decided to pull his small boat to shore and check for damages.

Being that he was on the far side of the lake and it was getting dark, he decided to camp for the night. After inspecting his boat and finding no damage, he felt that a fresh start in the morning would indeed be his best choice. He found a comfortable spot to camp, built a small fire, and fell asleep.

He was awakened by the sound of something he didn't recognize. It was a very loud shrieking sound. He quickly put out his fire, not wanting to call attention to himself.

The last thing he wanted was to come face to face with whatever was making that awful sound. But he grew more and more curious about the strange sound, so he decided to find out what it was. There was a full moon that night, so finding his way through the wooded area surrounding the lake was not too difficult.

The stranger came to a small clearing and peeked around a thick bush. He couldn't believe his eyes. There, dancing around a huge fire was the strangest looking little man that he had ever seen. He was small, but very powerful looking. He had beady eyes and a large nose. His body was hairy and his hands were enormous. The stranger couldn't help but to stare at its thick hairy neck. It looked like a small tree trunk. He knew what this thing was. It was a troll. He had seen one in a book of mystical magical creatures that he had bought for his son.

The stranger stood frozen to the spot

when, suddenly, the troll turned around and looked at the place where the man was hiding. He remembered reading that trolls have a very strong sense of smell. As luck would have it, a small animal scurried from between the stranger's legs, and the troll pounced on it. Satisfied that the animal was what he had smelled, he went on with his dancing.

After several turns around the fire, the troll sat down and started talking to himself. When the stranger heard what the troll had to say, he ran as quickly and quietly as he could back to the spot where he had left his boat. He wasted no time heading for the lights of the village to tell his story to anyone who would listen.

"What was it that the stranger heard?" asked Hope and her mother almost at the same time.

James went on to tell them that, of course, nobody wanted to believe what the stranger had said. They thought he was suffering from too much sun or too little water to drink. But he insisted that that wasn't the case and that he knew what he saw and heard was true.

The man said that the troll was bragging about something that he had done that day. He started out by screaming into the fire that this was his lucky day and that it wasn't every day that a troll made a deal with a mermaid. James said that when the stranger talked about the troll, he described him as being mad or insane, explaining that he talked to the fire, telling his story as if the mermaid or something was sitting right there with him. The troll danced around in happiness as he recalled the moment that the mermaid agreed to the deal to save her sister.

The stranger said the troll was babbling on and on, talking about following Misty the Wish Fairy to Ireland, wanting to ruin her plan to grant a wish! However, as he was flying over Lake George, he suddenly saw something come flying up out over the waves. It was a beautiful creature. It was green and scaly, and the scales were green, blue, and gold. As they caught the sun's rays, they looked like hundreds of tiny diamonds. Her eyes were a beautiful sky blue and had very wide, wide long lashes. Her hair looked like spun gold and was in a long thick braid hanging down her back.

But of all these beautiful features, it was her crying that captured his attention. It was strong and loud, but it sounded like music to his ears. He landed on the shore and waited to see if he would catch a glimpse of her again. He didn't have to wait long.

She appeared out of the water like a dream and draped herself over a large, flat rock near the water's edge. He could see that the mermaid was very nervous and had already started to cry again. Being the evil troll that he was, he felt no sympathy for her. However, excitement raced through his body as she started to plead with him.

"Please, sir, can you help me? My sister's tail is trapped between two of the rock shelves in the cove, and I tried and tried but I can't get her out. You look very powerful. Will you help me free her?"

The troll realized his opportunity. "And what will you do for me?" screeched the troll. The mermaid slid back further on the rock when she heard the terrifying sound of his voice.

"What do you request? If you are willing to help us, we need to do this soon. We mermaids get our life's nourishment from the algae and tiny lichen that grow on the rocky ledges. We were searching for food when her tail got stuck. There are only two of us here now, and we have to watch out for each other." The deal the mermaid was about to make would change her life and her sister's.

"This is what I want." The stranger, who continued to watch, said at this time he almost left out of fear at the anger in the troll's voice. "I want you make a deal with me that if I save your sister you will help me in whatever I ask you to do until my mission is complete."

"Well, sir, what is it that you are going *to* want me to do? We mermaids are a very gentle people with gentle ways and, unlike the tales that people tell about us, we do not want to do harm to sailors or anyone else. We just want to live in peace until my sister and I can find our way back to the warm seas where we come from."

"ENOUGH!" shrieked the evil troll. "My mission is none of your concern. Do you want my help or not? I can kill your sister as easily as I can save her. Now! WHAT IS YOUR ANSWER?" After the mermaid agreed, he knew what he had to do to put his plan in place.

The villagers say that on the night of the deal, people for miles around could hear what sounded like a sad song of regret coming from the lake. The troll turned her into a creature and forced her to appear in the water, scaring the tourists into leaving out of fear.

Next he started trapping a lot of the fish so that the tourists had no fish to catch. He thought this was a genius move on his part. His plan worked out exactly like he wanted it to. Most of the fish were trapped, the tourists were being scared away by the creature, and THE GRANDPOP AND ME FISHING EXCURSION business was losing a lot of money.

When James finished his story, he looked around at his friends. Hope had a sick look on her face and was shaking, and Hope's mother was just staring straight ahead with her mouth wide open. "What is wrong, my friends? Please do not be frightened. The story I have told you is just a fishermen's tale. There has never been any proof that the mermaids or the troll really exist. As far as the monster in the lake goes, like I said, it could be just a huge fish that had been trapped in the rock shelf and has since freed himself."

"Oh, no, James," said Mary Catherine. "It is not just a tale. We know of this evil troll you talk about. Hope and Misty have dealt with him in the past. Hope was part of the group that led to the troll being held prisoner by the giants."

Hope spoke up, "Holy Fairy Dust, Mom. I have to find Misty — and fast."

But there was more to the story that James, Greg, and the village did not know. The evil troll stayed in the area until the storm passed. As he was flying over the lake, near the far end away from the curious eyes of the village, he spotted a damaged boat that he knew was Greg's grandfather's because of the close encounter he had earlier. That same boat passed within a very short distance of where he spotted the mermaid for the first time. He smiled to himself, because now he knew what he had to do!

Using black magic, he guided another boat that had been tipped over on its side by the wind into the ELIZABETH and clapped loudly when the mast plunged into the side leaving a huge hole.

Now, the troll hoped that Greg would need to call upon Misty, his Wish Fairy, for help and this is when he would defeat her. The hurricane type storm was just a bonus and fit in wonderfully with his evil plot. In the meantime, he turned the mermaid into the horrible creature when she refused to do any more of his evil work, and kept her hidden in a cage, like a trophy, until he returned from Ireland.

This is an original drawing by the author's 8 year old grandson, Michael. It is his vision of the monster in the lake.

Unfortunately for Misty and Hope, the troll had returned to Lake George! He had been flying back from Ireland when he stopped to rest and check on his creature. He got angry when he remembered that, until recently, he had been held prisoner by a group of giants. As a favor to Misty (oh, how he disliked that Wish Fairy), they had put him in a cage surrounded by chamomile plants, which are a troll's worst enemy. For some reason, trolls lose their power near these plants.

One day the giants went off on a hunting trip and left him by himself. He couldn't believe his luck when a freak storm came and washed the plants down the mountainside. He was then able to use his power to escape.

However, knowing that Greg's

grandfather's boat was so badly damaged, the troll laughed and knew Greg would call on his Wish Fairy to help them. He would stick around to make sure Misty's plans were ruined and the wish not granted!

Not knowing if Misty realized the troll was already here, Hope looked all over for her friend to tell her. Not being able to find her, she went back to the house. In her room, thinking, Hope had an idea. Maybe Misty would be keeping out of sight near the library. "She knows that I love to go there." She had hoped that Misty would come to the house last night but, unbeknownst to Hope and Mary Catherine, her mother's friend hosted a welcome back party for them. It seemed like most of the town was there.

The next morning, Hope hopped out of bed, got dressed, and told her mom she was off to find Misty. Her mother insisted she have some breakfast. After grabbing a freshly baked blueberry scone off the platter, Hope went running towards the door. "Hold on there, Honey," said Mary Catherine. "You need to promise me that you will be extra careful now that we know the troll may be in the area. I don't think that he will try anything in broad daylight, but you never know with that evil little man."

"I know. I will be extra special careful but, Holy Fairy Dust, Mom, I have to find Misty and warn her."

"I know, Honey. Just come and give me a big hug and kiss and off you go." Hope did not go far before she got the familiar feeling that came over her every time Misty was nearby.

After listening to James' story, Misty barely made it back to her hiding place. It was in an abandoned birdhouse in the tree next to the library. She was shaking so hard she could hardly fly. The troll was back. How did this happen? Then her fear turned to anger. What was he doing here and what was he after? She knew the answer. He wanted HER! Did he know about Greg's wish?

Misty wanted so badly to talk to Hope last night, but when she arrived at the house it was full of people. There was a party going on, and she didn't want to risk being seen yet. She had no choice but to fly back to the birdhouse and hope that her friend would come looking for her. And she did. Misty looked out of the little opening of the birdhouse just as Hope came walking down the street towards the library. Misty felt better already.

At home, Hope's mom decided to visit James. She wanted to bring him and Greg some of the scones she had made. She hoped that they would have the chance to talk some more. Greg was not around, but she found James near his boat, cleaning out some of the wood that had fallen inside the cabin. The boat ended up full of debris when the other boat crashed into it. "Good morning, James. How are you this beautiful morning? I brought you and Greg some breakfast."

"Good morning, Mary Catherine. Greg is not here. He is off reading up on the Biggest, Bestest Fish Contest. The town has just finished putting up the posters for it. But those scones sure smell good. Come, sit down. I just made some coffee."

The friends sat down, side by side, drinking their strong coffee and enjoying their scones. "So, do you want to talk?" Hope's mom asked.

"Sure," said James.

He started off by telling Mary Catherine what they saw when they stepped outside after the storm. The hurricane type storm was over. He said that when the wind stopped howling, he grabbed Greg by the hand and walked up the cellar stairs. There were already a lot of people standing outside the bait and tackle shop where they had taken cover. When he saw the way people were staring and pointing their fingers, he knew that it wasn't good. He said, "I was right. It wasn't good. The main street was devastated. The storm had turned Main Street into a river of mud. Signs were down, fences were broken, benches were tossed around, and flowers and small bushes were uprooted. But the thing that devastated me the most was the harbor."

James said that one of the first things he noticed was the lake. It looked like chocolate milk in a blender. The water was swirling around in whirlpools. As the waves washed up onto the shore, they brought with them pieces of wood from boats that had been crashed into by other boats due to the high winds and waves. Amazingly, some boats were hardly touched. Other boats were flipped upside down, some had gaping holes in their hulls, and some were completely destroyed.

One of those boats, he was sad to say. was his boat: the ELIZABETH.

"Oh, James, I am so sorry. Do you have any idea how much it is going to cost to repair and to make it totally seaworthy?"

"Yes, I had it looked at by a friend of mine who worked as a ship builder before coming here to live. He said it is going to cost anywhere from ten to fifteen thousand dollars to make her totally seaworthy again."

"Oh, that is so much money. No wonder Greg called upon his Wish Fairy for help."

"I don't think that even a Wish Fairy can help me now. With no insurance, I will never be able to raise that much money. Everyone who believes in fairies knows that a Wish Fairy cannot grant a wish by handing out money."

"You are right about that James, but don't you worry. Misty will do everything in her power to see that you and Greg get back in business."

After sitting with her friend a little longer, Mary Catherine went back to the house to wait for Hope.

Misty made sure that no one was watching and quickly flew over to Hope, landing on her arm. (It was Misty's favorite place to ride.) "Hi, Misty, it is so good to see you," said Hope. "Now, let's get down to business, and you can tell me what you are going to do about the troll and this wish that you are going to try to grant."

"I thought I was going to fall out of the flower box I was hiding in when I heard James say that they thought the troll was involved with the so-called monster in the lake. It took me so by surprise."

"Me too," said Hope. "I should have known he would figure out a way to escape."

"The troll still thinks that he has the power to stop me from granting wishes. Well,

THAT will never happen. I will never allow such an evil creature to destroy the wishes of innocent people," said Misty.

"So what are we going to do?"

"You, Hope, are not going to do anything at this time. I do not know what we are dealing with and, until I do, I would like you to please stay here and watch over Greg."

"I will do whatever you ask," said Hope.

Misty said that she needed to try and make contact with the monster in the lake. She tried to make Hope understand that because she, too, was a mystical creature, that maybe she and the creature could find a common bond. But this thing could be very dangerous. She just didn't know. She flew off telling Hope that she would let her know how the meeting with the creature went.

Meanwhile, in the deepest, darkest part of the lake, the troll was quite alive and well. He was plotting his scheme of how to stop

Misty. When he escaped Ireland and his prison, he threw a listening spell to the wind. This was a one-time spell, and he had been saving it up for just the right moment, and this was it. The spell worked by placing an enchantment on one person. Through this enchantment, you could hear what they were saying, but for only a short period of time. Lucky for him, the spell lasted long enough to hear Greg's wish to Misty.

It took all of Misty's belief in magic to give her the courage to dive down into that lake. Fairies are not great swimmers. In fact, they hardly swim at all. Some of the castle keepers would dive into the lake where Misty's favorite lily pad was located. They dove down to collect the beautiful conch shells that lay on the lake bottom. They were used for decoration when the Queen hosted a celebration.

Misty sure wished that one of the divers

were here now. She knew she would be fine, though. Breathing under water was one of the things that she was trained to do when she was appointed Wish Fairy.

The water was dark and dirty. She could see little bubbles coming from the air pockets between the rock shelves. It was while she was resting on one of these shelves that she heard it. She froze in her tracks. Misty would know that sound anywhere. It was the sound of the troll shrieking, and he sounded happy.

But wait, what was that other sound? It was very odd and musical, but sad. She needed to get closer to see what was going on. She hid in one of the cracks on the rock shelf. The little fairy was not prepared for what she saw; in fact, she couldn't believe her eyes.

The troll was not alone. In a large wire cage, partly submerged in one of the large pockets of waters caused by a runoff of lake water from the stone ledges, was probably what the villagers called the monster of the lake. It was a horrible looking thing, but it had such a sad expression on its ugly face that Misty couldn't help but feel sorry for it.

"So the stories are true," Misty thought to herself. Before she realized what was happening, the troll waved his thick hairy arm over the creature and started to chant.

"ONCE A MERMAID, FAIR AS CAN BE, NOW THIS CREATURE, BELONGS TO ME."

The creature started to spin around in the cage faster and faster until Misty could hardly see it. When it stopped spinning, the creature was gone and, in its place, lay the most beautiful mermaid she had ever seen.

The mermaid opened her mouth as if to speak. The troll screeched at her to be quiet. He told her she knew the consequences if she refused to obey him again. He said he was going to leave the cave for a short time, and he would bring her back some food. In the meantime, she was to keep her mouth shut so as not to call attention to herself if there happened to be any fishing boats in the area. Misty waited patiently for the troll to leave. She knew he would not be gone long, and she needed to find out as much as she could.

Very slowly, she swam toward the mermaid. "Hello," she said. "Please do not be afraid of me. I just want to talk to you."

"Who are you?" asked the mermaid.

"My name is Misty, and I am a Wish Fairy. I need you to tell me what the troll has been up to and if you know what he is planning to do. You see, he has been trying to stop me from granting wishes for a very long time. The wish I am trying to grant is for a small boy named Greg, and it is a very important wish. Won't you please talk to me?"

The mermaid nodded her head, and as she tugged at her long braid, she began to explain how she came to be trapped in this cage by the troll. It was quite a story. Because they were both afraid that the troll would come back and catch Misty, they decided to meet again the next day.

Misty flew immediately to where Hope was anxiously waiting for her. She told Hope and Mary Catherine the disturbing story that the mermaid told her. Misty started to speak, and it was so quiet that you could hear a pin drop.

One beautiful day, the mermaid and her sister were swimming peacefully in a small lagoon where the water was warm. Close by, under the sea, was the mermaid kingdom that they knew and loved. The mermaids knew every fish and every creature in the lagoon, and they were as happy as could be. All of a sudden, a strange current started pulling them out of the lagoon. The mermaid hung on to her sister's tail as they were pulled along to a strange new world.

The water was different. It was cold and dark in spots and had rock ledges where huge fish lived. There were dry caves with large pockets of water. They shivered as they tried to get used to this new climate that they found themselves in. They had no idea where they were or how they got there.

The mermaid I spoke to said she begged her sister to stay close, but she wouldn't listen. She wanted to explore the rock ledges that surrounded this strange new world. Her sister swam in and out among the rocks, not realizing the danger. Before the mermaid had time to warn her sister, it was already too late. She was trapped.

For a while, she said, neither of them panicked. Then, all of a sudden, they realized how much trouble her sister was in. Not only was she trapped on a rock ledge, but there was a large air pocket right above her head. The way she was trapped, she could not get her head into the water. Mermaids cannot stay out of the water for long periods of time. They need to be able to totally submerge themselves in order to survive. If the mermaid didn't get her sister out of there soon, she would die. This is when she met and asked the troll for help.

Realizing that her sister was running out of time, she agreed to make a deal with the evil little man. Once the deal was made, explained Misty, the troll freed the sister, but banished her to an unknown place.

"Holy Fairy Dust!" exclaimed Hope. "That poor mermaid was no match for the troll."

Misty continued, saying the troll knew all about Greg's wish because of the clever listening spell cast. In fact, he also knew about the damaged boat, because he was the one that helped cause the damage in the first place. Oh, yes, the hurricane type storm did do some damage, but the Elizabeth was a sturdy boat, and she wasn't going to need a lot of repairs. The troll had to do something. He needed the boat to be damaged enough that Greg and his grandfather would not be able to pay to have it fixed. He needed Greg to call upon his Wish Fairy for help, and that is exactly what he did.

When Misty finished telling her story, Hope said, "Can we do anything to help her?"

"I have been thinking about this, and I am sure that there is a reversal spell that I can use. I am not quite sure of the ingredients, and I have to use the right one or we could all be in trouble. But I know someone who knows the spell well and has used it many times."

"Who is it?" asked Hope. "Maybe they can help us."

"It is my mom," said Misty proudly.

Hope told Misty that tomorrow she and her mother had to drive home because her mother had a follow up doctor's appointment that she could not miss. Before coming to Lake

George, she had stepped on a rusty nail and it got infected. The doctor wanted to make sure that the antibiotic was working.

"This could work out fine, Hope. Would you be able to contact my mom and ask her to give you the reversal spell? I know that she has used it before and knows what it is."

"I can do that, but are you sure she will give it to me?"

"Hope," pleaded Misty, "this is very important. I am counting on you to do this for me. I do not want to make a mistake and make things worse for the mermaid. You have always come through for me before, and I am sure you will again."

Hope went back to the house and told her mother what Misty had asked her to do. "That is a fine idea, but how are you planning to get in touch with Misty's mother."

"Well, Mom, if we can get back to the wildflower field before the babies leave the surface, then I can have one of them take my message to Misty's mother. I am sure that she will help us. They can tell her where and when to meet me."

"Alright, then, Hope. You better get to bed so we can get an early start in the morning."

Hope put on her favorite lake pajamas (the ones with the multi-colored fish on them), and went out on the porch where her mother was drinking tea and looking up at the stars. She sat for a minute and stared at the beautiful blue mountain towering over the lake. She stood up and gave her mother a great big hug like she didn't want to ever let her go. She whispered in her mother's ear how sad she felt for the mermaid.

"I'm sure it is very hard for her to be without her family and not know where her sister is or if she is ok. Poor monster/mermaid that is trapped beneath the water, MY HEART

JUST ACHES FOR YOU!"

"Don't worry, Hope. You and Misty will figure it out. You always do."

"Holy Fairy Dust, Mom. I hope you are right."

Mother and daughter hugged and kissed good-night. "Now, go to bed, Hope. You have a very important job to do tomorrow."

Misty knew that she just couldn't sit around and wait for Hope to return with the spell. She dove back into the water and again went to the spot where the mermaid was trapped. She had to wait quite a while for the troll to leave. Thank goodness she had that small air pocket.

When he finally left, Misty showed herself once more to the mermaid. This time, the evil little man had left her in the creature form. "Can you recognize me? Do you remember who I am?" asked Misty.

The creature replied, "Yes, Misty. It is only my body that has taken on this terrible form. My mind has always remained the peaceful mermaid."

Misty explained to her that they had a

plan, and they were going to help her escape. The creature said that she had some news that might be helpful. "I know that you must have dealt with the troll in the past, so you know that he likes to talk to himself. Well, I heard him saying what a fool I was. He hadn't banished my sister to some far away sea. She was very close by in a small cove not far from here."

Misty left the creature with the promise that she would go and find her sister and would return with news.

The little Wish Fairy couldn't help but notice the one fish that was swimming close to shore. He looked different than the other fish. (Misty knew how that felt.) She decided to try to talk to him. "Hello there," said Misty. The fish flopped around a little bit, shot up into the air, spun around, and plopped back down into the water.

"What are you trying to do? You almost

scared the scales off me. It is not every day that someone talks to me, you know."

"I am sorry that I scared you. I mean you no harm. Let me introduce myself."

"I know who you are. The lake fish have been talking about you since you arrived. Are you and that human child going to put things back to normal around here?"

"I am certainly going to try," said Misty.

"Cool! My name is Fred, and I am not a happy fish these days. I have been trapped and released by that hairy little troll more times than I can count. The other fish are saying that you are the reason the troll is here in the first place. Is that true?"

"Sadly, yes," replied Misty. "He is trying to prevent me from granting a very important wish for the little boy named Greg who lives on the other side of the lake."

"Hey, I know Greg. He is that nice kid that throws small pieces of biscuits into the water. I'll bet you didn't know that fish like biscuits, did you? Why, that hairy old sack of nothing good troll. What can I do to help get rid of him?"

Misty asked Fred if he knew of any cove where the troll may be hiding a mermaid. He said he did and told Misty to follow him. They had only gone a short distance when Misty saw the beautiful mermaid swimming just a little bit below the water. She saw Misty and Fred and immediately lifted her head out of the water. Misty explained what was going on and asked the mermaid what was holding her captive and why didn't she just swim away. Misty could not see any chains or vines, and there was no sign of a cage.

"The troll put an invisible captive spell on me so that I am unable to leave this cove."

"Well," said Misty, "that is one spell that I am able to break." With a flutter of her tiny wings and a nod of her head, Misty had set the mermaid free. Misty told the mermaid that she would go and tell her sister that she was free. She also told her that it was very important that she try to find her way home so that no further harm could come to her. Misty could see that she was a much smaller and younger mermaid than her sister and hoped that she had the wisdom to find her way home.

"Wait, wait, wait!" yelled Fred, jumping in and out of the water. "I can help. I can help. I can lead her. I know the way." Misty couldn't believe her ears. Fred knew the way out. What a wonderful miracle. After promising the young mermaid that she would tell her sister she was safe, she hurried back to where the creature was waiting for her.

The creature was clearly agitated. It kept slamming its body into the sides of the cage, trying to get free. Misty was terrified that the creature was going to hurt itself.

"Stop, stop, please," cried Misty. "I

know that you are upset and you want to get out of here, but I have some good news for you. I have set your sister free, and she is on her way home." The creature raised its ugly head, and Misty could see the tears pouring down from its eyes.

"Thank you, Misty. I don't know how I could ever repay you for this act of kindness. You are a true Wish Fairy. I have been wishing for my sister's release from the moment the troll made us prisoners."

"You can thank me by not banging your head against the cage again." That brought what looked almost like a smile to the creature's face.

The creature told Misty that she had some bad news to tell her. The troll was going to be releasing all the fish in time for the contest, and he is saving the biggest fish as bait for Greg.

"What do you mean, 'bait for Greg'?"

"I am not sure, but I am sure that it can't be good.

Misty left the creature with the promise of returning soon and flew back to her birdhouse by the library to wait for news from Hope.

Misty saw a lot of activity everywhere. There was a new excitement in the air. Then she realized what it was all about. The fishing contest, of course. There were posters on every lamppost and banners hung from the shop windows.

A big sign was put up outside the town hall that read:

COME ONE, COME ALL
LAKE GEORGE BIGGEST, BESTEST FISH CONTEST!
$20,000.00 CASH PRIZE FOR THE 1st PLACE WINNER!
ALL ARE WELCOME!
REGISTER AT THE BAIT AND TACKLE SHOP!

"Oh, no," said Misty. "Things are really moving fast around here." Questions flooded the little Wish Fairy's mind. Where is Hope?

Did she get the spell? Was she even able to get the message to my mom? And the most important question of all: I wonder what that troll is up to!

Hope's mom had barely stopped the car before Hope jumped out and headed straight for the wildflower field at full speed. The sun had just started to rise, and Hope was worried that she had missed the babies. They were only allowed to stay on the surface long enough to make sure that the flowers had all they needed to bloom. Once the sun rose, they were to return to their kingdom.

Most of the babies had gone below, but Hope spotted two of them changing the color of a daffodil from gold to yellow. "Wait!" she hollered, as the babies were ready to dive below the ground. "It is me, Hope, and I need to talk to you. Please wait, it is very important. I have a message from Misty."

Both of the fairies stopped in their

tracks. "Hi, Hope," said the babies in their squeaky little voices. "What is the message and who is it for?"

"It is for Misty's mom. Will you make sure that she gets it?"

"Yes, of course, anything to help Misty."

"Good, then tell Misty's mom to meet me under the big oak tree in the center of the wildflower field. Tell her that it is the same one where we had our meeting before." Hope watched as the babies dove underneath the ground. I hope Misty's mom gets the message, and we have time to meet before we have to drive back to the lake.

Just when Hope thought that Misty's mom was not coming, she heard the flutter of tiny wings and knew that it was her. The fairy looked very concerned as she flew over to where Hope was sitting. She asked Hope what was wrong and if Misty was ok. Hope told her that Misty needed the spell that would change the creature back into a mermaid. Misty's mother said that she would give it to her, but Hope was going to have to give her a few minutes to make up the potion. She told Hope to stay right where she was, and she would return shortly.

Hope paced up and down, waiting for Misty's mom to return. Mary Catherine joined her daughter, and together they waited. They saw the glow before they saw the fairy. The small bottle that Misty's mom held in her hand was glowing like the silver dust that fell from an angel's wing. She handed Hope the bottle and told her to be very careful with it and do not attempt to open it. It was enchanted and to be opened only by Misty.

"Holy Fairy Dust," thought Hope. "In my hand I have the power to change a creature into a mermaid." Hope's mom gently tugged on her arm and told her daughter that they would have to hurry if they were going to get the bottle to Misty. Hope said good-bye to Misty's mom and ran behind her mom to the car.

They arrived at the lake a little after 3:30 that afternoon. The town was busy. People were getting ready for the fishing contest. Women were sweeping their store fronts and were putting out brightly striped chairs for people to sit on. Teenage boys were placing trash barrels out, encouraging the tourists not to litter, and the men were replacing any broken glass and changing the bulbs in the streetlamps.

Greg's mother, Marlene, was in the kitchen busy making fish chowder and biscuits. They were going to need a lot to be able to feed the large amount of fisherman and spectators. Greg sadly walked into the kitchen and hugged his mom around her waist. "Oh, Mom," he said. "My Wish Fairy told me to enter the fishing contest and that maybe I would catch the biggest, bestest fish ever. But, what if I don't? Grandpop will never get his boat repaired."

"Greg, Honey. First, none of this is your fault. You are not responsible for the lack of business, your grandfather canceling the insurance, and for sure you are not responsible for the hurricane type storm. You have done everything that a boy of your age could possible do. I think now that you have decided to call upon your Wish Fairy, you should put your trust and faith in her. She said she would do everything in her power to grant your wish, didn't she?"

"Yes," he sighed.

"Then maybe you should enjoy being in the fishing derby and leave the rest to Misty."

"OK, Mom. I think I will."

Misty was quite confident that Hope would succeed in bringing her the spell. And with her mother making the potion, she knew that she would be able to change the creature back into the beautiful, mystical mermaid. She knew that this was important, but it was Greg's wish that she had to concentrate on. Little did she know just how connected these two things were.

Misty saw Hope running down the street with the bottle held tightly in her hand. Out of breath from running, she quickly handed the bottle to Misty. As Misty was getting ready to fly away, she told Hope to go back to the house and wait. She said that she would come to her and tell her what happened. Misty thanked her friend and told her that she would see her soon, and off she flew into the sky that was becoming darker by the moment. She really wanted to change the creature back before dark and was very afraid that the troll would realize that the younger mermaid was gone.

As Misty got closer to the cage, she could hear voices. Her heart sank as she realized that the troll was there. It wasn't the mermaid or the creature that he was talking to— it was the fire. He glared into the flames and said out loud, "I have released all the fish back into the lake. Soon the lake will be full of boats, and everyone will be after the prize fish. What these fools don't know is that only I know where the biggest and bestest fish is. He is hidden so well that no one (not even that pesky Wish Fairy, Misty) will ever find it. He is resting comfortably on one of the stone ledges. I have to make sure that Misty will never find it, or that bratty kid may win the $20,000 and ruin my plan to defeat Misty."

Misty stood frozen as a statue when the troll spun around and frantically looked in her direction. "WHAT IS THIS THAT I SMELL? IS SOMEONE THERE?" he screeched.

Luckily, at that same moment, the creature also spotted Misty and knew it had to do something to distract the troll. She raised her short stubby arm and threw a rotting fish in the direction of the troll. "So, this is what smells." He threw the fish back at the creature and made his way out of the watery cave.

Misty did not know how long he would be gone or how long it was going to take for the potion to work. She knew that if she was going to grant Greg's wish, she needed to finish this before the little evil man returned. Misty told the creature to move closer to the front of the cage.

Giving the creature two thumbs up, Misty opened the small bottle, and sparks of every color started shooting out of the cap. Misty was stunned. She had never seen anything like this before. She raised the bottle and poured it over the head of the creature. And to her shock and disbelief, NOTHING HAPPENED!

Tears slid down the little fairy's face as she watched the monster slither to the back of the cage. I am so sorry. I will think of another way to turn you back. I promise. She didn't think the creature heard her.

It wasn't until she was flying to the house to talk to Hope that it came to her like a flash of lightning why the potion didn't work. It couldn't be carried by a human unless the transporting spell was released. And Misty's mom forgot to take it off. She couldn't believe this stroke of bad luck.

"Holy Fairy Dust, Misty," said Hope. "I hope it was nothing that I did."

"No, Hope, the potion comes with a spell that only the person doing the transforming can take the lid off. The other part of the enchantment is there to make sure that the potion doesn't end up in the wrong hands. My mother just forgot to take it off. Don't feel bad. We will think of some other way to save the mermaid."

"We better think of something fast. Tomorrow is the fishing contest, and once you grant Greg's wish, there is no telling what the troll will do to the mermaid creature." Misty said she understood and gave Hope her instructions for tomorrow.

Hope was to stay on the dock with Greg while he was fishing and to keep her eyes open in case the troll showed up. He may try to harm Greg. If she saw him, she was to pull Greg off the dock and into the coffee shop. There is chamomile tea there, and the troll would never go anywhere near it. The two friends said goodbye, and Misty flew off to try and find Fred, the fish.

Misty knew that if anyone would know where the troll was keeping the biggest, bestest fish ever, it would be another fish. She flew back and forth across the area of water where she first met Fred. There was no sign of him. Then out of the corner of her eye, she spotted him doing his Fred thing, jumping in an out of the water, spinning around, and plopping back down into the water.

"Fred, Fred," she called out softy, just in case the troll was nearby.

"Hi, Misty. I brought your little friend out to the island and, from there all she had to do was cross under the channel into the ocean. I watched her as she swam farther and farther out to sea."

"That's great, Fred, but I need to talk to

you about something really important. Do you have any information about where the troll is hiding the biggest, bestest fish?"

"Of course I do, silly. Not much has been going on in these parts for the last 50 years that I don't know about. Do you want me to show him to you? I visit him nearly every day and twice on Sunday."

"You don't say," laughed Misty. "Go right ahead and lead the way." And Fred, the fish, did just that.

The little fairy was not prepared for the size or color of this fish. It was enormous. She could not have even guessed at the weight or length. It would for sure bury the weights, as the fisherman would say. The body of the fish was a silver color with stripes running lengthwise across his massive body. Its scales were bright colors that seemed to change with his surroundings. The more he moved around, the more the colors of his scales changed. He truly was the biggest and bestest fish ever. Here it was, swimming right in front of her, the $20,000 fish! Misty saw Fred swim over to the huge fish. It looked like he was talking to it.

"Fred, are you talking to that fish?"

"Well, yes, of course I am. Did you honestly think that I am the only fish in this lake that is able to hear and speak?"

"I really didn't have a chance to think about that. Are there many more of you?"

"Only a few. But we don't mind, do we, Fishy? That's what I like to call him, Fishy."

Fred told Misty that he and Fishy had quite a conversation. He said that Fishy never said a word when the troll was around, because he doesn't like him enough to talk to him. Plus, he doesn't take kindly to being stuck in such a small swimming area. Fishy said that this morning the troll came to check on him and said, "Well, you big piece of shark bait. Tomorrow I will set you free. When the fishing contest is over I will banish you from this lake forever."

"Well, let me tell you. Fishy was not happy. He told me that no one was going to banish him from the home he lived in since he was a tiny fish."

Misty asked Fred if Fishy knew about Greg's wish, and he said, yes, that he had told him. Fishy said he would try to swim as close as he could to where the boy was fishing, but it was going to have to be up to Greg whether or not he hooked him. The boy had to want to win the contest with his whole heart and needed to do whatever it took to make it happen. Misty said that her job was to make sure that Greg was in an area where there were not too many people fishing.

She thanked the fish and asked him if he believed in magic. He told Misty, of course, he did. How else would he be able to talk and hear if it weren't for magic? As she was flying away, she realized that Fishy was right. She could only help and show him the way, but Greg was going to have to land that fish himself. She was making the wish possible for him. If he proved himself worthy, then it would be granted.

Misty knew that she was going to have a hard time sleeping, but she had to try and get some rest. She was going to grant Greg's wish, and figure out how to change the creature back into a mermaid and how to make sure that no harm came to Fishy. Whew! It was going to be a long day.

Meanwhile at the house where Hope and Mary Catherine were staying, things were very quiet. There was nothing that Hope really wanted to do, and she knew that she was going to have a hard time sleeping. She had just come in from the porch where she and Greg had eaten some delicious sweet watermelon that Mary Catherine had cut up for them.

They talked about the contest

tomorrow, and Hope told Greg what Misty had said they were to do should the troll appear. He agreed that he would stay close to Hope. Earlier, they had walked along the lake and found the perfect spot to fish. The water was deep but warm, and also crystal clear. In fact, Hope said it was like looking into a mirror. Greg told her that was because it was a cove that was fed by a stream coming off Blue Mountain.

He got very quiet all of sudden, and Hope asked him what was wrong. He told Hope that he was worried about his grandpop. Ever since he has been unable to take the boat out, he had become very depressed. She told Greg not to worry, that Misty would not let him down. She just hoped that she was right.

Hope found her mother in the kitchen, cleaning up the mess from the watermelon. Hope said, "Mom, you know Greg is really a wonderful boy. He told me tonight that if he caught the fish and won the contest, his plan was to release the fish back into the lake as soon as they weighed it."

"Oh, you mean he doesn't want to cut it up and fry it up and share it with the whole village?"

"Holy Fairy Dust, Mom! Are you kidding me? He would never do that."

"Of course, I am kidding, Hope. Now get ready for bed. I have a feeling it is going to be a big day tomorrow."

Hope laughed, kissed her mom, and went straight to bed. She had hoped that maybe Misty would pay her a visit tonight, but it didn't happen. Unable to keep her eyes open another minute, Hope fell fast asleep.

After some tossing and turning and almost getting caught by someone who wanted to take the birdhouse out of the tree, Misty, too, fell asleep. She woke up to the sights and the sounds of a village filled with excitement.

They were people everywhere ready to fish. There were wonderful smells of coffee brewing, bacon frying, and scones baking. People were sitting on picnic tables and benches and blankets — anywhere they could find a spot. And the weather was beautiful — warm, sunny, and not a cloud in the sky.

After picking at some tiny berries that she found growing on a bush, Misty immediately took off to speak to the creature. Luckily, the troll was not there. She told the creature that when the troll released her, she was to do exactly as he said, but don't try to escape. Misty explained that she may need her to help defeat the troll. Misty then went off to talk to Fred and Fishy. She also gave them instructions as to what she wanted them to do.

Misty needed to see her friend Hope. Hope had played such a huge part in helping Misty to grant some of her other wishes that talking to her best friend always made the fairy feel better. It gave Misty confidence to know that Hope had so much faith in her. No matter what problem Misty was faced with or how much danger was involved, she could always count on Hope being there for her.

Hope was waiting for Misty on her window seat. The friends talked for a while until Misty said, "I have to go now, Hope. Please try not to worry. I am, after all, a Wish Fairy, and a good one at that. I appreciate all the help, and it is important that you know, I WILL grant this wish." With a wave of her tiny arm, she was gone.

Hope knew that she had to get moving. Greg was going to pick her up in half an hour. She still had to eat breakfast and get dressed. It was going to be a warm day, so she jumped in the shower, put her hair in a ponytail, and put on her favorite shorts set. She wanted to wear her sneakers, so it took her a little time to find her lucky socks. On them were written, FAITH, HOPE, and LOVE. She had just enough time to finish her blueberry pancakes and drink her juice when Greg showed up.

It was obvious from the look on his face that Greg was nervous. Mary Catherine hugged them both and told Greg to forget about the prize money and just do what he loves — fish. Everything will then become much easier. Hope and Greg walked hand in hand down to the dock. Greg had his favorite fishing pole slung over his shoulder. As she watched them go, Mary Catherine whispered to the sky.

"Please, to anyone that may be listening to me, I do believe in magic and I know that those two kids do too. Please make everything turn out alright today."

She walked back into the house to pack some things to take with her down to the dock to watch the contest. Stepping onto the porch, she looked up to the sky once more and said, "Did I say thank you?" Because at that moment a feeling came over Hope's mother so strong that she knew everything was going to be alright. She found a seat next to James, and together they waited for the contest to begin.

Suddenly they heard the countdown: 5-4-3-2-1 FISH! The contest had started! There was no turning back now for any of them. Mary Catherine and James watched as hundreds of fisherman casted their lines into the water. A short distance away she could see Hope and Greg. They watched as Greg pulled his arm back and perfectly cast his lure into the water.

It was a lure that his grandfather had helped him make. James told Greg that it was a good sturdy lure. He remembered that they were sitting on the bench outside the bait and tackle shop. They both laughed so hard they couldn't stop, when James said to Greg, "Hey, buddy, if you don't land a big one with this lure, I will eat my hat."

This memory brought a big smile to Greg's face. This was one lure he was going to keep forever. After a few fish swam around his line, he began to lose hope of catching the big one. Suddenly, Hope tapped him on the arm and pointed to the water.

Swimming toward them was the biggest fish that they had ever seen. It was a beauty. Greg slowly and surely cast his line into the lake. The fish was so big that Greg was afraid that his line would not hold. His grandfather had filled his reel for him, and no one knew more about fishing than him, but still he felt his palms start to sweat.

Greg was also worried that, even if he was lucky enough to hook this fish, would he be strong enough to reel him in? He didn't have much time to think about it, because that fish bit right down on that lure. Hope backed out of the way to give Greg more room. Everyone on the dock stood up and watched. They could see that Greg had hooked one huge fish.

Inch by inch, Greg reeled him in. What surprised the boy was that the fish didn't put up too much of a fight, which was ok with Greg. Just as he snapped his wrist back to land the fish, something terrible happened. He was distracted by something that was flying through the air toward him. He was so nervous and his hands were so clammy that he watched in horror as his pole, precious lure, and huge fish went sliding back into the lake.

Then Greg and Hope heard it — a loud

screeching sound. Hope had no time to react. The troll flew through the air at top speed and pulled the fish, line, and pole right out of the water with him.

Greg stood on the dock with tears pouring down his face. He made a split second decision. He couldn't just stand there and watch his dream of fixing his grandfather's boat disappear. Without a second thought for his own safety he screamed, "NOOOOOOOOO! Give me back my fish! You cannot have it. It is mine and my grandpops. I need that prize money." Before anyone knew what was going on, the little boy dove into the deep water. He started to swim after the pole but soon realized he wasn't a strong enough swimmer. Greg started to go under.

As Hope raced to get help, someone else was also watching the boy. The creature and Misty were both on the other side of the lake. The creature was such a strong swimmer that it knew it would get to the boy faster than anyone else. People's eyes were suddenly drawn to the horrible creature racing through the water. Through the haze in its eye, the creature could see the sheriff standing on the shore with a large net and tranquilizer gun.

They were going to try and shoot the creature to knock it unconscious. The creature, Misty, and Hope all realized at the same time that the sheriff thought the creature was going after Greg to hurt him. Greg was just about to go under for the last time. He just couldn't swim any more, when the creature reached him.

Hope raced to the sheriff and begged him not to shoot. She explained that the creature wasn't trying to hurt Greg, it was trying to save him. He lowered his gun just as the creature dove down underneath Greg, slicing its face on a sharp rock, not caring about its own life and safety. As it shot back up out of the water, loud screams of shock came from the people on shore. This was no monster. This was a beautiful mermaid. The creature's act of unselfish love and kindness reversed the spell and turned her back into the beautiful sea creature that she was. She swam to shore with Greg safe in her arms and laid him gently on the sand. He opened his eyes and smiled at her. "Thank you, beautiful lady, for saving my life." The mermaid smiled, left him, and swam toward where the troll and the fish had landed in the lake.

Misty had beaten her to it. As soon as she saw that Greg was ok, Misty also took off after the troll. She was just about to reach him when he shot up out of the water with the fish and pole in his hairy little hand. The troll was in such a hurry to get away that he didn't realize he was flying so low. Misty knew what was about to happen and flew on up ahead near the rocky ledges. She stood with her hands on her hips so the troll could see her. While the troll was busy looking at Misty and wondering what she was up too, Fred did what Fred does best. He jumped out of the water, spun around, and pulled that fish, pole, and lure right out of the troll's hand. Fred swam to shore, pulling Greg's pole behind him. He was headed toward Greg, who was now sitting up and watching.

The troll was just about to follow them when Misty cried out in her loudest voice, "Here I am, you coward! You pick on small children and innocent sea creatures but, if I am the one that you want, why don't you come and get me? Or maybe you are too afraid?"

One of the things that Misty remembered about trolls was that they do not like to be known as being afraid of anything or anybody. The troll looked at Misty and thought to himself, "There she is. All I have to do is go and destroy her. This tiny fairy cannot defeat me or my powers. I can get rid of her once and for all."

On the shore, people began running toward Greg. By the time anyone got there, Greg was sitting peacefully on the grass with the huge fish hooked to his line, swimming in the water. The officials checked Greg over and, deciding that he was ok, took the fish to be weighed.

Greg ran alongside them soaking wet and met up with Hope, Mary Catherine, Marlene, and James. They all walked together to the weighing station where the fish were being placed on a large scale.

There were many big and beautiful fish there, but none could compare to the one that Greg caught. Everyone was so happy and, although no one had said for sure who the winner was, they all knew in their hearts that it was Greg.

Yes, everyone was very happy and

excited, except for Hope. Because she still didn't know what was going on between Misty and the troll.

Misty knew at once that her plan had worked. The troll was flying straight towards her, and his beady eyes were flashing red. He was furious, which was exactly what the little fairy wanted. You see, when trolls got angry, really angry, they got sloppy and they let their guard down. They can focus on one thing and one thing only and, for this troll, he was focused on Misty.

His plan had always been to defeat her and stop her from granting wishes. Yes, he was furious that Misty, and what he liked to call that horrible human child friend of hers, had beaten him in the past, but not this time. This time, it is just me and her, he thought. Misty cannot out power me. I am so much stronger than her.

Misty knew that she had a lot of people counting on her, and she would not let them down. She knew that what she was doing was dangerous, but it needed to be done. Misty had to keep moving because, if he threw a spell at her, she would be helpless. Yes, the troll was powerful, but so was she. She had all the knowledge of the fairy kingdom within her, and she would count on all that they taught her. Maybe she could not physically beat him, but she could mentally beat him.

As the troll got closer, she knew what she had to do. She started flying in a zigzag pattern. In and out she flew between the wide rock shelves, being careful not to let him get too close. He was right behind her now. She knew it was going to have to be now or never if her plan was going to succeed.

She dove into the cove where the troll had kept the mermaid prisoner. The rock shelves there were much smaller. She knew that she would have no trouble getting through them, and she also knew that the troll's big thick hairy body could easily get stuck like the mermaid's sister did. And THAT was her plan all along.

In and out, and in and out, she flew with the rock ledges getting narrower and narrower. The troll was so blinded by rage that he wasn't even aware what was going on right in front of him. Misty stopped just a few feet from where he was. He was panting and out of breath, but he was so excited to think that soon, very soon, he would have his revenge.

One more time, Misty thought to herself, one more time is all I need. She slipped into a small air space between the rocks and waited. At first, the troll seemed to be thinking about it, but then he just flew headfirst into the space between the rocks, pinning his arms to his sides. The last thing Misty saw as she escaped through a tiny crack in the back of the shelf was the fury in the troll's face.

"You will be sorry, Misty! You wait and see! You will be sorry," screeched the troll.

It was one happy Wish Fairy that flew back to shore. She could see them all lined up on the dock watching and waiting for her. And right there in front, jumping up and down and waving her arms, with a huge smile on her face, was her best friend, Hope. Misty and Hope hugged each other as much as a tiny Wish Fairy and a little human girl could. Then it was time for the big question. "Did I do it, Hope? Did Greg catch the biggest, bestest fish ever?"

"I don't know, Misty. Let's go. They are going to make the announcement any time now."

"Wait, Hope. I have to find the mermaid and thank her."

"I am right here, Misty, and it is I who needs to thank you. You have saved my sister and me."

"It was my pleasure, and thank you for saving Greg. Wait, what happened to your face?"

"Oh, I sliced it on a rock when I dove down to rescue Greg. I wasn't paying attention. That is a mermaid hazard, you know, swimming around those rocks."

"Well, I can certainly take care of your face. I have my own powers, you know, granted to me by my Queen, only to be used when absolutely necessary. And this is one of those times." Misty very softy ran her fingers over the cut on the mermaid's face and magically, of course, the injury was gone, and her face was just as beautiful as ever.

"Hurry," said Hope. "Look, they are about to make the announcement."

The friends, Misty, Hope, Mary Catherine, James, Marlene, the mermaid, and even Fred, listened very nervously to the man at the microphone. "It is with great pleasure that we announce the winner of THE BIGGEST BESTEST FISH CONTEST with the prize being a check for $20,000. This year's winner is Greg from the Grandpop and Me Fishing Excursion team."

"Holy Fairy Dust!!" screamed Hope. "You did it, Greg, you did it. Yay!" Mary Catherine looked over at James and, as he hugged his daughter and grandson, a single tear slid down his cheek. He knew for the first time in months that everything was going to work out for them.

As the townspeople and tourists started to pack up, Misty noticed something unusual in the water. She couldn't quite make out what it was, but then the mermaid shouted for joy. "Look! It is my sister and some people from my kingdom. They have come to lead me back to my home."

And there, right in the front of the group of mermaids, was Fred. He looked over at

Misty and said, "Hey somebody's got to show them the way home, and who better than me?"

After saying goodbye to her new friends, the mermaid jumped into the water and joined her family. And, as for Fred, he shot out of the water, spun around, plopped back into to water and headed for the channel that led to the open sea.

It was starting to get dark, and people were getting into their cars to go home when, all of a sudden, the sky exploded with hundreds of beautiful fireworks. The mayor had come over to congratulate Greg when James said, "Beautiful fireworks, Mayor. That was a nice end to the day."

"Thank you," smiled the mayor, but I had nothing to do with this. This show has nothing to do with me. Hope looked at Misty, and they both knew. The Queen was sending Misty a message. They wanted her to know that they were proud of her and that she did a great job of granting this wish.

The summer flew by after that, and James got his boat repaired in time for the fall excursions. Misty flew home to check her basket in case there was another wish in there. Hope and her mom spent the rest of their time at the lake, swimming, boating, and relaxing. Hope and Greg continued to be good friends and spent a lot of time together.

On the week before they were due to go home, Hope, Mary Catherine, and Marlene all went berry picking. They made jam and jelly, and there were plenty of berries left for Marlene to make scones. Greg's family bought the bait and tackle shop from the owner who was retiring. James hired someone in town to run it, and Marlene turned the basement into a charming little café and bakery.

On their last night at the lake, they all shared a beautiful dinner of fish chowder and biscuits with homemade blueberry jam and chamomile tea. The owner of the coffee shop could not figure out why once a week James would stop by and pick up two bags of chamomile tea and take it out with him on the boat. Then he would simply drop it into the lake near the rock ledges and leave.

They were all standing on the dock, one last time, before Hope and her mom left. They hugged, and said their goodbyes with promises to return next summer. As Hope was turning to leave, something landed on her arm. "Misty! Holy Fairy Dust, is it really you?"

"Yes, I have come to tell all of you something that is very important to me. Yes, I was the one who granted the wish, but I could not have done it without the help of my friends, and for that I want to say thank you." Everyone needs help sometime, even if you are a Wish Fairy with a best friend named Hope.

About the Author

Sandra has been creating and telling stories to her children and grandchildren for many years. From scary stories around a campfire to heart-warming bedtime stories, she has instilled the belief in magic to many young minds.

Her goal is to not only get children to read but, more importantly, to see and feel the magic found within the pages.

Sandra was born and raised in Utica, New York, and currently lives there with her husband Jeff. Her life, centered around family and friends, is full of magical times and magical food!

About the Illustrator

Dominique has her Masters of Science by Research degree from the University of New South Wales, Australia, and is currently pursuing her doctorate in Chemistry.

She lives in upstate New York.

For more information about

Misty the Wish Fairy

and her friend Hope

visit

www.sandrareilly.com

and remember to always

BELIEVE !

Look for these other books in the

Wish Fairy Collection !

 The Wish Fairy

 The Basket of Wishes

 The Cottage Down the Lane
with the Dragon Out Back

 Oops, Where Did I Put That Star?

 A Valentine for My Daddy

 What's at the End of the Rainbow? Nothing!

 The Sunny Day, Rainy Day Ride